CLASSICS
Illustrated ®

Charles Dickens
GREAT
EXPECTATIONS

essay by
Michael Doylen, M.A.
The Dickens Project
University of California at Santa Cruz

ACCLAIM BOOKS
STUDY GUIDE

Great Expectations

art by Henry Keifer

Classics Illustrated: Great Expectations
© Twin Circle Publishing Co.,
a division of Frawley Enterprises; licensed to First Classics, Inc.
All new material and compilation © 1997 by Acclaim Books, Inc.

Dale-Chall R.L.: 6.75

ISBN 1-57840-011-2

Acclaim Books, New York, NY
Printed in the United States

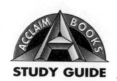

STUDY GUIDE

GREAT EXPECTATIONS

By Charles Dickens

PIP

MRS. JOE

JOE GARGERY

MAGWITCH

COMPEYSON

MISS HAVISHAM

ESTELLA

MR. JAGGERS

HERBERT

HIS FAMILY NAME WAS PIRRIP, BUT ALL WHO KNEW THE BOY CALLED HIM PIP FOR SHORT, ENTIRELY FORSAKING HIS FIRST NAME OF PHILLIP. TO THE VILLAGERS OF THE MARSH COUNTRY DOWN NEAR THE RIVER, WHICH WOUND TWENTY MILES TO THE SEA, HE WAS POINTED OUT AS THE BROTHER OF MRS. JOE GARGERY WHO MARRIED THE BLACKSMITH. IT WAS EXPECTED THAT PIP WOULD FOLLOW HIS BROTHER-IN-LAW'S CALLING. NO ONE EVER EXPECTED HE WOULD BECOME A YOUNG MAN OF GREAT EXPECTATIONS, LEAST OF ALL, PIP HIMSELF. AS THE ORPHANED SON OF PHILLIP AND GEORGIANA PIRRIP, IT WAS DEEMED FORTUNATE FOR THE BOY THAT HE HELD THE AFFECTIONS OF THE HONEST BLACKSMITH AND HIS LOVING BUT SHREWISH WIFE. NEVER HAVING SEEN EITHER OF HIS PARENTS, IT WAS PIP'S PLEASURE AT TIMES TO TAKE HIMSELF TO THE VILLAGE CEMETERY AND THERE TO INDULGE HIS FANCIES IN WHAT THEY WERE LIKE.

PIP AND HIS BROTHER-IN-LAW, THE BLACKSMITH, WERE GREAT FRIENDS. IT MAY HAVE BEEN BECAUSE THEY WERE FELLOW-SUFFERERS OF THE SHREWISH MRS. JOE GARGERY.

MRS. JOE HAS BEEN OUT A DOZEN TIMES LOOKING FOR YOU, PIP! AND WHAT'S WORSE, SHE'S GOT A CANE WITH HER.

PIP, SHE'S A COMING! GET BEHIND THE DOOR, OLD CHAP!

TELL ME WHERE YOU'VE BEEN, YOU YOUNG MONKEY!

I HAVE ONLY BEEN TO THE CHURCHYARD!

IF IT WASN'T FOR ME, YOU'D HAVE BEEN TO THE CHURCHYARD LONG AGO AND STAYED THERE! WHO BROUGHT YOU UP BY HAND?

YOU DID!

I'D NEVER DO IT AGAIN. YOU'LL DRIVE ME TO THE CHURCHYARD BETWIXT YOU TWO. OH, A PRECIOUS PAIR YOU'D BE WITHOUT ME!

IT WAS CHRISTMAS EVE, SEATED AT THEIR EVENING MEAL, THE GARGERYS AND PIP WERE SUDDENLY STARTLED BY THE NOISE OF A CANNON FIRING . . .

THERE WAS A CONVICT ESCAPED LAST NIGHT AND THEY FIRED WARNING OF HIM. NOW, THEY'RE FIRING WARNING OF ANOTHER.

WHO'S FIRING?

DRAT THE BOY! WHAT A QUESTIONER HE IS!

MRS. JOE, WHERE DOES THE FIRING COME FROM?

FROM THE HULKS!

HULKS ARE THE PRISON SHIPS, PIP. RIGHT ACROSS THE MARSHES!

IN DARKNESS, PIP CLIMBED THE STAIRS TO HIS BED IN MORTAL TERROR OF THE CONVICT HE MUST MEET AT DAWN. .

I WONDER WHO'S PUT INTO PRISON-SHIPS?

PEOPLE ARE PUT IN THE HULKS BECAUSE THEY DO ALL SORTS OF BAD; AND THEY ALWAYS QUESTIONS. NOW, YOU GET ALONG TO BED!

DAWN FOUND PIP STEALING SOME BREAD, CHEESE AND A BOTTLE OF BRANDY TO TAKE TO THE GRAVE-YARD

A HASTY VISIT TO THE FORGE AND HE FOUND THE FILE WHICH THE CONVICT DEMANDED . . .

SWIFTLY, PIP MADE HIS WAY THROUGH THE MIST TOWARDS THE CHURCHYARD IN ORDER THAT HE MIGHT RETURN BEFORE MRS. JOE NOTED HIS ABSENCE . . .

PIP CAME UPON ANOTHER CONVICT . . .

IT MUST BE THE YOUNG MAN THE OTHER ONE SPOKE ABOUT.

PIP AWAKENED THE CONVICT TO GIVE HIM SOME OF THE FOOD, BUT THE ALARMED CONVICT STRUCK AT PIP AND DISAPPEARED INTO THE MIST . . .

PIP RAN TO MEET THE OTHER CONVICT...

WHAT'S IN THE BOTTLE, PIP?

BRANDY.

I THINK YOU HAVE GOT THE FEVER.

I'M MUCH OF YOUR OPINION!

YOU'VE BEEN LYING ABOUT THE MARSHES AND THEY'RE DREADFULLY FEVERISH.

I'LL EAT MY BREAKFAST BEFORE THEY'RE THE DEATH OF ME. I'D DO THAT IF I WAS GOING TO BE STRUNG UP TO THE GALLOW DIRECTLY AFTERWARDS.

THE CONVICT GOBBLED THE FOOD, STARING DISTRUSTFULLY AT PIP AS HE DID SO, AND STOPPING ONLY TO LISTEN FOR SOUNDS...

YOU'RE NOT A DECEIVING IMP? YOU BROUGHT NO ONE WITH YOU?

NO, SIR! NO!

I BELIEVE YOU.

AREN'T YOU GOING TO LEAVE ANY OF THE FOOD FOR HIM?

HIM? WHO'S HIM?

THE YOUNG MAN YOU SPOKE OF, THAT WAS HID WITH YOU.

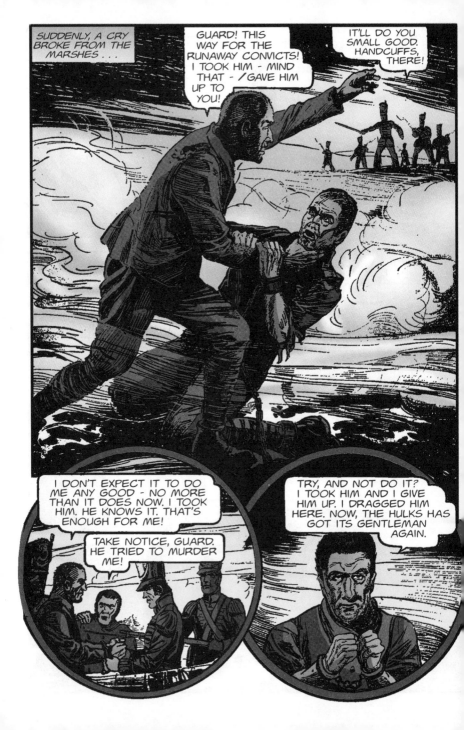

FOR THE FIRST TIME, THE CONVICT NOTICED THAT PIP WAS AMONG HIS CAPTORS . . .

ENOUGH OF THIS! LIGHT THOSE TORCHES!

PIP HAD BEEN WAITING TO CATCH THE CONVICT'S EYE THAT HE MIGHT ASSURE HIM OF HIS INNOCENCE IN THE CAPTURE. HE SHOOK HIS HEAD SLIGHTLY AND THE CONVICT UNDERSTOOD HIM . . .

I WISH TO SAY SOME THING RESPECTING THIS ESCAPE!

YOU CAN SAY WHAT YOU LIKE BUT YOU HAVE NO CALL TO SAY IT HERE!

THIS IS ANOTHER MATTER. I TOOK SOME VITTLES UP AT THE VILLAGE YONDER, FROM THE BLACKSMITH.

BLACKSMITH, HAVE YOU MISSED ANY ARTICLES OF FOOD?

HE'S WELCOME TO THEM. WE DON'T KNOW WHAT YOU'VE DONE, BUT WE WOULDN'T HAVE YOU STARVED TO DEATH FOR IT, WOULD US, PIP?

NO, JOE!

ONE DAY, PIP WAS TAKEN BY HIS UNCLE PUMBLECHOOK TO THE HOME OF THE RICH, ECCENTRIC OLD LADY, MISS HAVISHAM. THERE, THEY WERE GREETED BY AN ATTRACTIVE YOUNG GIRL ABOUT PIP'S AGE.

WHAT NAME, PLEASE?

PUMBLECHOOK, AND THIS IS PIP!

THIS IS PIP, IS IT? COME IN PIP, I AM ESTELLA.

DON'T BE RIDICULOUS, BOY. I AM NOT GOING IN!

GO IN, BOY!

ESTELLA HAD DISMISSED PUMBLECHOOK AND NOW, SHE LED PIP TO MISS HAVISHAM'S FORBIDDING ROOM.

AFTER YOU, MISS!

ANYTHING ELSE?

VERY INSULTING!

SOON, THE GAME CAME TO AN END AND PIP FOUND HIMSELF DISMISSED WITH THE REMINDER TO RETURN TO THAT GLOOMY HOUSE IN SIX DAYS...

ESTELLA, TAKE HIM DOWN AND LET HIM HAVE SOMETHING TO EAT.

ESTELLA INSOLENTLY GAVE PIP SOME BREAD AND MEAT. BY HER MANNER, PIP FELT LIKE A DOG IN DISGRACE...

WHY DON'T YOU CRY?

BECAUSE I DON'T WANT TO!

YOU DO AND YOU ARE NEAR CRYING NOW!

THE FOLLOWING DAY, PIP CALLED AT THE "THREE JOLLY BARGEMEN" TO MEET JOE AND THERE MET A STRANGER...

YOUR SON?

NO!

NEPHEW?

NO!

PIP WAS SUDDENLY STARTLED AS THE STRANGER WINKED HIS EYE AND THEN DISPLAYED A FILE TO STIR HIS GLASS - IT WAS THE VERY FILE PIP HAD TAKEN TO THE CONVICT IN THE CHURCHYARD...

MR. GARGERY, I HAVE GOT A BRIGHT, NEW SHILLING, AND THE BOY SHALL HAVE IT.

'TIS VERY GOOD OF YOU, SIR.

THE STRANGER TOOK HIS LEAVE OF JOE AND PIP BUT NOT BEFORE HE HAD PRESSED SOME CRUMPLED PAPER INTO PIP'S HAND...

IT'S TWO POUNDS!

HE MUST HAVE MADE A MISTAKE. I'LL GO AFTER HIM!

ONE EVENTFUL DAY, SEVERAL YEARS LATER, MRS. JOE WAS ATTACKED BY AN UNKNOWN INTRUDER AND BEATEN ABOUT THE HEAD. TO NURSE HER BACK TO HEALTH, THEIR FRIEND, BIDDY, WAS BROUGHT TO THEIR HOME. HOWEVER, SHE WAS NEVER TO RECOVER HER SPEECH, OR BE OTHERWISE WELL AGAIN. IT WAS THUS THAT BIDDY CAME TO THE GARGERY HOUSEHOLD . . .

BIDDY IS PLEASANT AND SWEET-TEMPERED

BIDDY AND PIP HAD MANY TALKS TOGETHER . . .

BIDDY, I WANT TO BE A GENTLEMAN.

OH, I WOULD NOT IF I WAS YOU. YOU ARE HAPPIER AS YOU ARE.

I'M DISGUSTED WITH MY CALLING AND MY LIFE.

I ONLY WANT YOU TO DO WELL AND BE COMFORTABLE.

WELL, I NEVER CAN BE UNLESS I CAN LEAD A VERY DIFFERENT LIFE THAN THE ONE I LEAD NOW AS JOE'S APPRENTICE.

THAT'S A PITY.

IF I COULD HAVE SETTLED DOWN, I MIGHT HAVE GROWN UP TO KEEP COMPANY WITH YOU. I SHOULD HAVE BEEN GOOD ENOUGH, SHOULDN'T I, BIDDY?

YES.

INSTEAD OF THAT, SEE HOW I GO ON. WHAT WOULD IT MEAN TO ME BEING COARSE AND COMMON IF NOBODY HAD TOLD ME SO.

WHO SAID IT?

THE BEAUTIFUL YOUNG LADY AT MISS HAVISHAM'S AND I WANT TO BE A GENTLEMAN ON HER ACCOUNT.

TO SPITE HER OR TO WIN HER HAND?

I DON'T KNOW!

IF ONLY I COULD GET MYSELF TO FALL IN LOVE WITH YOU, BIDDY!

BUT YOU NEVER WILL, YOU SEE!

BECAUSE I THINK YOU WOULD SPITE HER BEST BY CARING NOTHING FOR HER WORDS. IF IT IS TO GAIN HER, I THINK SHE IS NOT WORTH IT!

IT WAS IN THE FOURTH YEAR OF PIP'S APPRENTICESHIP THAT A STRANGER APPEARED, ONE EVENING, AT "THE THREE JOLLY ARGEMEN . . ."

I HAVE REASON TO BELIEVE THAT THERE IS A BLACKSMITH AMONG YOU NAMED JOSEPH GARGERY.

I AM YOUR MAN.

YOU HAVE AN APPRENTICE NAMED PIP?

I AM HERE!

MY NAME IS JAGGERS AND I AM A LAWYER IN LONDON. I WISH TO HAVE A PRIVATE CONFERENCE WITH YOU TWO.

TAKING THE LAWYER TO THEIR HOME, JOE AND PIP WERE AMAZED AT JAGGER'S OPENING REMARKS . . .

I AM THE CONFIDENTIAL AGENT OF ANOTHER. WOULD YOU WANT ANYTHING TO CANCEL PIP'S INDENTURES FOR HIS OWN GOOD?

NO.

NOW, I TURN TO THIS YOUNG FELLOW AND THE COMMUNICATION I MAKE IS THAT HE HAS GREAT EXPECTATIONS.

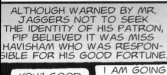

ALTHOUGH WARNED BY MR. JAGGERS NOT TO SEEK THE IDENTITY OF HIS PATRON, PIP BELIEVED IT WAS MISS HAVISHAM WHO WAS RESPONSIBLE FOR HIS GOOD FORTUNE.

WELL, YOU'RE QUITE A FIGURE, PIP!

I HAVE COME INTO GOOD FORTUNE, MISS HAVISHAM, AND I AM GRATEFUL FOR IT.

YOU? GOOD GRACIOUS, WHAT DO YOU WANT?

I AM GOING TO LONDON, MISS POCKET, AND I WANT TO SAY GOODBYE TO MISS HAVISHAM.

HER INSTRUCTIONS TO KEEP THE NAME OF PIP WAS ONE OF THE TERMS SPECIFIED BY JAGGERS. PIP WAS MORE THAN EVER CONVINCED THAT MISS HAVISHAM WAS HIS BENEFACTOR. HIS YOUNG HEART OVERFLOWED WITH GRATITUDE FOR WHAT HE CONSIDERED THE OLD WOMAN'S ANONYMOUS GENEROSITY . . .

I HAVE SEEN MR. JAGGERS AND HEARD ABOUT IT. YOU ARE ADOPTED BY A RICH PERSON -- NOT NAMED -- AND YOU WILL ALWAYS KEEP THE NAME OF PIP. GOODBYE, PIP.

GOODBYE, MISS HAVISHAM.

PIP RODE ALONG IN THE LONDON COACH TO HIS NEW LIFE, BUT HIS HEART REMAINED AT HOME WITH JOE AND BIDDY . . .

IN LONDON, PIP VISITED THE OFFICE OF MR. JAGGERS AND THERE HE MADE A VALUABLE ACQUAINTANCE IN MR. WEMMICK. THE LAWYER'S CLERK . . .

MR. JAGGERS IS IN COURT AT PRESENT. AM I ADDRESSING MR. PIP?

YOU MUST BE MR. WEMMICK.

MR. WEMMICK SUGGESTED THAT PIP CALL ON THE LAWYER LATER; AND THAT MEANTIME, HE SHOULD SECURE LODGINGS WITH HERBERT POCKET.

DO YOU KNOW WHERE MR. POCKET LIVES?

AT HAMMERSMITH, ABOUT FIVE MILES WEST OF LONDON.

THE MONTHS PASSED AND PIP'S EDUCATION AS A GENTLEMAN PROGRESSED. HE ACQUIRED MORE CULTIVATED TASTES AND HIS AMBITION WAS STIRRED BY HERBERT'S KNOWLEDGE OF BUSINESS . . .

WHEN I HAVE MADE MY CAPITAL, I SHALL TRADE TO THE EAST INDIES FOR SILKS, DYES, AND SPICES.

ARE THE PROFITS LARGE?

TREMENDOUS!

PIP LEARNED THAT HERBERT NEEDED MONEY TO SET HIM UP IN BUSINESS. . .

IS YOUR JOB IN THE COUNTING-HOUSE PROFITABLE?

NOT DIRECTLY. IT DOESN'T PAY MUCH AND I HAVE TO KEEP MYSELF.

BUT THE THING IS, IN A COUNTING-HOUSE YOU CAN LOOK ABOUT YOU AND ONCE YOU HAVE YOUR CAPITAL, YOU CAN EMPLOY IT.

A FEW WEEKS LATER, PIP RECEIVED A NOTE. HE HAD NEVER SEEN THE HAND-WRITING BEFORE BUT KNEW AT ONCE WHO HAD SENT IT...

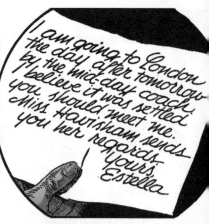

I am going to London the day after tomorrow by the mid-day coach. I believe it was settled you should meet me. Miss Havisham sends you her regards. Yours Estella

PIP KNEW NO REST OR PEACE AND HAD NO APPETITE UNTIL THE DAY ARRIVED WHEN ESTELLA WAS DUE IN LONDON...

WHEN IS THE COACH DUE?

FOUR OR FIVE HOURS.

ESTELLA SEEMED MORE DELICATELY BEAUTIFUL THAN EVER IN PIP'S EYES...

I AM GOING ON TO RICHMOND AND YOU ARE TO TAKE ME. FIRST, I WILL TAKE SOME TEA AND REST AWHILE.

A CARRIAGE WILL BE SENT FOR, ESTELLA.

HOW DO YOU GET ALONG WITH MR. POCKET?

AS PLEASANTLY AS I COULD LIVE ANYWHERE AWAY FROM YOU.

HOW CAN YOU TALK SUCH NONSENSE? NOW, TAKE ME TO RICHMOND.

PIP WISHED HE COULD ESCAPE FROM THE ROOM AS THE QUARREL CONTINUED . . .

DID I NEVER GIVE HER LOVE! LET HER CALL ME MAD.

WHY SHOULD I CALL YOU MAD, I OF ALL PEOPLE? DOES ANYONE LIVE WHO KNOWS WHAT SET PURPOSE YOU HAVE ONE HALF AS WELL AS I DO? WHEN HAVE YOU FOUND ME FALSE TO YOUR TEACHING? WHO TAUGHT ME TO BE PROUD? WHO PRAISED ME WHEN I LEARNED MY LESSON? WHO TAUGHT ME TO BE HARD? WHO PRAISED ME WHEN I LEARNED MY LESSON?

THE MISERABLE MISS HAVISHAM HAS NOW LEARNED THAT ESTELLA HAS NO LOVE FOR HER . . .

WOULD IT BE WEAKNESS TO RETURN MY LOVE?

I MUST BE TAKEN AS I HAVE BEEN MADE.

PIP SLIPPED QUIETLY FROM THE ROOM AND FROM THE HOUSE . . .

WHEN HE REACHED HIS TWENTY-THIRD BIRTHDAY, PIP HAD MADE IT POSSIBLE FOR HERBERT POCKET TO ENTER A BUSINESS PARTNERSHIP WITH SOME OF THE MONEY HE RECEIVED FROM MR. JAGGERS . . .

PIP WAS STARTLED ONE DAY BY A NOISE IN THE HALLWAY . . .

IS THERE ANYONE DOWN THERE?

YES!

WHAT FLOOR DO YOU WANT?

THE TOP, MR. PIP.

WHAT IS YOUR BUSINESS?

AH, YES, MY BUSINESS. I WILL EXPLAIN IT IF I MAY COME IN.

THAT'S MY NAME. IS THERE ANY-THING THE MATTER?

NOTHING THE MATTER!

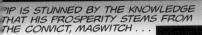
PIP IS STUNNED BY THE KNOWLEDGE THAT HIS PROSPERITY STEMS FROM THE CONVICT, MAGWITCH...

FROM THAT THERE HUT AND THAT THERE HIRING-OUT, I GOT MONEY LEFT ME BY MY MASTER AND GOT MY LIBERTY AND WENT FOR MYSELF. IT ALL PROSPERED WONDERFUL!

IT WAS ALL FOR YOU, PIP AND THE GAINS OF THE FIRST FEW YEARS I SENT HOME TO MR. JAGGERS-- ALL FOR YOU. DIDN'T YOU THINK IT MIGHT BE ME?

NEVER, NEVER!

THROUGH MOST OF THE NIGHT, PIP HEARD THE DETAILS OF MAGWITCH'S RISE TO FORTUNE IN THE PENAL COLONY...

MY FRIEND IS ABSENT- YOU MUST USE HIS ROOM.

LOOK HERE, DEAR BOY, CAUTION IS NECESSARY!

HOW DO YOU MEAN, CAUTION?

IT'S DEATH FOR ME TO COME BACK. I SHOULD BE HANGED IF TAKEN. I WAS SENT FOR LIFE.

AS MAGWITCH SLEPT, PIP LOOKED ON HIM WITH MIXED EMOTIONS. HE FEARED THAT AT ANY MOMENT, PURSUERS MIGHT BREAK DOWN AND TAKE THE MAN FOR HANGING AT OLD BAILEY PRISON...

NEXT MORNING. . .

I DO NOT KNOW WHAT NAME TO CALL YOU. I HAVE GIVEN OUT THAT YOU ARE MY UNCLE.

THAT'S IT, DEAR BOY, CALL ME UNCLE.

YOU ASSUMED SOME NAME ON SHIPBOARD?

YES, I TOOK THE NAME OF PROVIS.

WHAT IS YOUR REAL NAME?

MAGWITCH, CHRISTENED ABEL.

HOW ARE YOU TO BE GUARDED FROM DANGER?

THE DANGER AIN'T SO GREAT WITHOUT I WAS INFORMED AGAINST. WHO KNOWS I'M HERE? THERE'S JAGGERS AND THERE'S WEMMICK, AND THERE IS YOU.

THERE'S DISGUSTING WIGS CAN BE BOUGHT FOR MONEY, AND THERE'S HAIR POWDER AND SPECTACLES... AND WHAT NOT. OTHERS HAS DONE IT BEFORE.

BUT YOU SAID LAST NIGHT IT WAS DEATH!

AND IT IS DEATH. DEATH BY THE ROPE IN THE OPEN STREET, AND IT'S SERIOUS THAT YOU SHOULD FULLY UNDERSTAND IT! BESIDES PIP, I'M HERE BECAUSE I'VE MEANT IT BY YOU, YEARS AND YEARS.

HELLO, PIP-- OH!!!

QUIET! IT'S HERBERT!

MAGWITCH SWORE HERBERT TO SECRECY . . .

TAKE IT IN YOUR RIGHT HAND. KISS IT!

DO AS HE WISHES, HERBERT!

NOW, YOU'RE ON YOUR OATH, YOU KNOW, AND MAY YOU BE STRUCK DEAD IF YOU SPLIT ON IT!

THAT NIGHT, HERBERT AND PIP DISCUSSED WHAT WAS TO BE DONE FOR MAGWITCH. PIP TOLD HIS COMPANION THE STORY OF THE MEETING ON THE MARSHES AND OF THE SECOND CONVICT WHOM MAGWITCH HAD HELD FOR THE SOLDIERS . . .

THE FIRST AND MAIN THING IS TO GET HIM OUT OF ENGLAND. YOU WILL HAVE TO GO WITH HIM AND THEN HE WILL GO.

BUT HOW?

IF ONLY A PRETEXT COULD BE MADE OUT OF THAT OTHER CONVICT WHOM HE HATES!

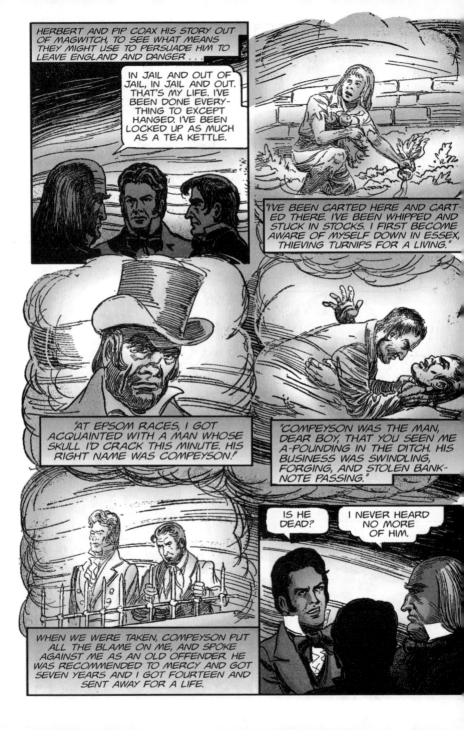

LATER, PIP LEARNS THAT ESTELLA IS BACK AT MISS HAVISHAM'S AND FOLLOWS HER . . .

WHAT BLOWS YOU HERE, PIP?

I FOUND SOME WIND HAD BLOWN ESTELLA HERE AND I FOLLOWED.

WHAT I HAD TO SAY TO ESTELLA, I WILL SAY BEFORE YOU. I AM AS UNHAPPY AS YOU EVER MEANT ME TO BE.

WELL?

HAVE FOUND OUT WHO MY PATRON IS. THERE ARE REASONS I MUST SAY NO MORE. WHEN I FELL INTO THE MISTAKE OF BELIEVING YOU WERE MY PATRON, YOU LED ME ON!

YES, I LED YOU ON!

WAS THAT KIND?

WHO AM I THAT I SHOULD BE KIND?

YOU MAKE YOUR OWN SNARES. I NEVER MADE THEM!

I SUPPOSE SO. IT WAS A WEAK COMPLAINT TO MAKE.

AT THIS POINT, ESTELLA ENTERED THE ROOM...

I AM GOING TO BE MARRIED TO DRUMMLE.

ESTELLA, I LOVE YOU. YOU KNOW THAT I HAVE LOVED YOU LONG AND DEARLY. I SHOULD HAVE SAID THIS SOONER, BUT FOR MY LONG MISTAKE.

ESTELLA, DO NOT LET MISS HAVISHAM LEAD YOU INTO THIS FATAL STEP. PUT ME ASIDE FOREVER, BUT MARRY ANOTHER THAN DRUMMLE.

WHY DO YOU INJUR OUSLY INTRODUCE TH NAME OF M MOTHER B ADOPTION? IT I MY OWN AC

SUCH A MEAN BRUTE, SUCH A STUPID BRUTE!

DON'T BE AFRAID OF MY BEING A BLESSING TO HIM! COME! HERE IS MY HAND. DO WE PART ON THIS, YOU VISIONARY BOY-- OR MAN?

RETURNED TO LONDON, PIP WAS STOPPED AT THE ENTRANCE TO THE HOUSE WHERE HE LIVED AND HANDED A NOTE BY A MESSENGER WITH A LANTERN...

WOULD YOU BE SO GOOD AS TO READ IT BY MY LANTERN?

PIP RECOGNIZED THE HAND-WRITING AS WEMMICK'S...

Don't go home!

MR. WEMMICK EXPLAINS TO PIP THAT COMPEYSON IS IN LONDON AND KNOWS THAT MAGWITCH IS HIDING OUT. COMPEYSON IS ONLY WAITING FOR A CHANCE TO DENOUNCE MAGWITCH TO THE AUTHORITIES. MEANTIME, A NEW HIDE-OUT HAS BEEN ARRANGED FOR MAGWITCH . . .

YOU HAVE BEEN WATCHED AND MIGHT BE WATCHED AGAIN.

PIP LEARNED THE ADDRESS OF MAGWITCH'S NEW HIDEOUT AND WENT THERE AT ONCE.

I HAVE TALKED WITH WEMMICK AND HAVE COME TO TELL YOU WHAT CAUTION HE GAVE ME AND WHAT ADVICE.

AY, AY, DEAR BOY!

IT IS AGREED THAT HERBERT AND PIP WILL GET A BOAT AND ROW MAGWITCH DOWN THE RIVER TO A PLACE WHERE HE AND PIP CAN EMBARK FOR EUROPE . . .

IT IS AGREED, WHATEVER YOU SAY, DEAR PIP!

DURING THE NEXT FEW DAYS, WHILE HE AND HERBERT SOUGHT TO GET A BOAT, PIP HAD A FEELING HE WAS BEING SPIED UPON . . .

I KNOW A BETTER COURSE THAN TAKING A THAMES WATCHMAN. TAKE STARTOP. HE'S A GOOD FELLOW, SKILLED HAND, AND HONORABLE.

HOW MUCH WOULD YOU TELL HIM, HERBERT?

HERBERT MENTIONED A FELLOW WHO WOULD HELP THEM . . .

VERY LITTLE, JUST LET HIM KNOW THERE IS URGENT REASON FOR GETTING YOU TWO ABOARD A FOREIGN STEAMER LEAVING LONDON.

WE'LL LIE QUIET DOWN-RIVER UNTIL WE CAN PULL OFF TO ONE.

WE'LL GO WHEREVER YOU SAY, PIP.

COMPEYSON CONTINUED TO HAUNT PIP'S FOOTSTEPS AS ARRANGEMENTS WERE MADE FOR THE HIRING OF THE BOAT . . .

EARLY MORNING, SAW PIP AND HIS COMPANIONS SHOVE OFF FOR DOWN-RIVER AND THE SHIP FOR HAMBURG . . .

A FOUR-OARED GALLEY WENT UP WITH THE TIDE A SHORT WHILE AGO! I DON'T LIKE IT!

DO YOU THINK IT WAS A CUSTOM HOUSE-BOAT, STARTOP?

IT COULD HAVE BEEN A CUSTOMS BOAT.

WE'LL BE SAFE IN ANOTHER HOUR AND PIP AND HIS UNCLE WILL BE ABOARD THE SHIP BOUND FOR HAMBURG.

HERE COMES THE STEAMER.

LOOK, THE GALLEY!

IT'S A CUSTOMS BOAT!

MAGWITCH AND COMPEYSON DISAPPEARED, LOCKED IN EACH OTHER'S ARMS.

THE STEAMER RESUMED ITS COURSE. PRESENTLY, A LONE FIGURE WAS SIGHTED SWIMMING NEARBY . . .

IT WAS MAGWITCH, SEVERELY INJURED FROM STRIKING HIS HEAD AGAINST THE KEEL OF THE STEAMER ON RISING . . .

COMPEYSON HAD DROWNED. PIP FELT A GREAT WAVE OF SYMPATHY FOR THE CONVICT WHO HAD FELT SO AFFECTIONATELY AND GENEROUSLY TOWARD HIM FOR SO MANY YEARS. PIP SENSED THAT MAGWITCH WAS SERIOUSLY HURT . . .

DEAR BOY, I'M QUITE CONTENT TO TAKE MY CHANCES. I'VE SEEN MY BOY AND HE CAN BE A GENTLEMAN WITHOUT ME.

SENTENCED TO HANG, MAGWITCH CHEATED THE ROPE BY DYING OF HIS INJURIES. PIP WAS AT HIS SIDE AT THE END . . .

O LORD, BE MERCIFUL TO HIM, A SINNER!

THE STATE CONFISCATED ALL OF MAGWITCH'S FORTUNE AND PIP BEGAN A NEW LIFE, WITH NEW EXPECTATIONS, AS HERBERT'S PARTNER IN BUSINESS . . .

HERBERT AND PIP BECAME VERY SUCCESSFUL ABROAD. PIP KEPT IN CONSTANT TOUCH WITH JOE, BUT IT WAS ALL OF ELEVEN YEARS BEFORE HE RETURNED TO HIS OLD HOME FOR A VISIT. THEY SPOKE OF ESTELLA...

TELL ME, AS AN OLD FRIEND, HAVE YOU QUITE FORGOTTEN HER?

I HAVE FORGOTTEN NOTHING IN MY LIFE THAT HAD A PLACE THERE... BUT THAT POOR DREAM, AS I ONCE CALLED IT, HAS ALL GONE BY.

BUT, PIP DECIDED TO REVISIT THE RUINED HOUSE WHERE HE HAD FIRST MET ESTELLA... MISS HAVISHAM HAVING LONG SINCE DIED...

ESTELLA!

I AM GREATLY CHANGED. I WONDER YOU KNOW ME!

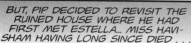

YOU HAVE ALWAYS HELD YOUR PLACE IN MY HEART.

SUFFERING HAS MADE ME STRONGER THAN ALL OTHER TEACHING AND HAS TAUGHT ME TO UNDERSTAND WHAT YOUR HEART USED TO BE. I HAVE BEEN BENT AND BROKEN; BUT I HOPE NOT OUT OUT OF SHAPE.

ESTELLA, NOW A WIDOW, AFTER A MOST UNHAPPY MARRIAGE, TOLD PIP THAT SHE NOW REALIZED, TOO LATE THE VALUE OF HIS LOVE...

I LITTLE THOUGHT I SHOULD TAKE LEAVE OF YOU ON THIS SPOT WHERE FIRST WE MET.

BUT LET US CONTINUE TO BE FRIENDS APART.

THEN PIP TOOK ESTELLA'S HAND IN HIS. AS THE MORNING MISTS HAD RISEN LONG AGO, WHEN HE FIRST LEFT THE OLD HOUSE, SO THE EVENING MISTS WERE RISING NOW, AND IN THEIR BROAD EXPANSE OF TRANQUIL LIGHT, HE SAW NO SHADOW OF ANOTHER PARTING FROM ESTELLA.

THE END

GREAT EXPECTATIONS:
CHARLES DICKENS

Charles Dickens was born on February 7, 1812 in Portsmouth, the second of John Dickens's eight children. In 1823, the Dickens family moved to London with the hopes of bettering their financial situation, but the family's plight quickly worsened. Twelve-year-old Charles began work at a blacking factory to help support the family when his father was arrested for debt, and the entire family—with the exception of Charles—moved into Marshelsea Debtors' Prison. At the blacking factory, Charles was paid six shillings a week; the work was tedious and the hours long (from twelve to fourteen hours each day). The misery of the experience haunted Dickens for the rest of his life. Three months after his imprisonment, John Dickens was released, and he soon sent young Charles to school. At fifteen, Charles taught himself shorthand so that he might work as a freelance reporter.

1836 was a landmark year for Dickens. It saw the publication of his *Sketches by Boz*, *The Posthumous Papers of the Pickwick Club*, and his marriage to Catherine Hogarth. *The Pickwick Papers* were an immediate success, and they made Dickens's reputation as a major novelist. The success of *The Pickwick Papers* was partly due to its serial publication. The novel—instead of being sold as one piece of work, as novels are today—was published in separate installments each month. Serial publication not only made novels less expensive for the average buyer, but they also had a built-in means of producing suspense. Between "parts," the reader was always left wondering what was going to happen next (the cliff-hanger effect was perhaps similar to the effect produced by soap-operas in our own day). Dickens followed *The Pickwick Papers* with a string of other successful, and still famous, works including *Oliver Twist* (1837),

At the Blacking Factory

Dickens deals with his experiences in the blacking warehouse in fictional form in David Copperfield, and the blacking warehouse itself appears ("offstage") in *Great Expectations*.

In a scene not shown in the Classics Illustrated adaptation, Joe visits Pip in London. When Pip asks Joe if he has seen anything of the city, Joe answers: "'Why, yes, Sir … me and Wopsle went off straight to look at the Blacking Ware'us. But we didn't find that it come up to its likeness in the red bills at the shop doors; which I meantersay,' added Joe, in an explanatory manner, 'as it is there drawd too architectooralooral.'" Dickens intends this to be a funny moment, but behind the humor lies a great deal of Dickens's own pain. It's the pain of a small child who feels himself abandoned by his family and his talents wasted in a horrible job. Dickens's pain is also expressed in Pip, who feels himself abandoned after the death of his natural mother and father and his talent wasted at the forge with Joe.

Nicholas Nickleby (1838-39), *The Old Curiosity Shop* (1840-41) and *A Christmas Carol* (1843). A second, more serious phase of Dickens's career as a novelist began in the late 1840s, with the appearance of *Dombey and Son* (1846-48). In this novel and the ones that followed it, Dickens was more critical than ever before of the injustices of English society. He showed a particular dislike for the British class system, which pitted the socially privileged against the socially deprived and so, Dickens felt, broke up the natural feelings of sympathy and good-will that humans otherwise have for each other. In the 1850s, he published *Bleak House* (1852-53), *Hard Times* (1854), *Little Dorrit* (1855-57), and *A Tale of Two Cities* (1859). *Great Expectations* (1860-61) was one of Dickens's final works. He published it in serial format in the pages of *All Year Round*, one of the magazines which he edited. His last novels were *Our Mutual Friend* (1864-65) and *The Mystery of Edwin Drood* (1870), which was unfinished at Dickens's death on June 8, 1870.

Pip is the protagonist of *Great Expectations*. The novel begins, "My father's family name being Pirrip, and my christian name Philip, my infant tongue could make of both names nothing longer or more explicit than Pip. So, I called myself Pip, and came to be called Pip." He and his sister, Mrs. Joe, are the only survivors of a family of nine. The novel tells of Pip's rise from apprentice to a blacksmith to gentleman in London.

Joe Gargery, his brother-in-law, is a "mild, good-natured, sweet-tempered, easygoing, foolish, dear fellow—a sort of Hercules in strength, and also in weak-

ness." Pip and Joe are "fellow-sufferers" under Mrs. Joe's "Ram-pages," as Joe calls them. Joe, in his own small way, tries to comfort Pip during the attacks of Pumblechook and Mrs. Joe.

THE WEARING OF THE DAY BROUGHT CHRISTMAS DINNER WITH THE GARGERYS' ANNUAL GUESTS, INCLUDING JOE'S UNCLE, MR. PUMBLECHOOK ...

BE GRATEFUL, BOY, TO THEM WHICH BROUGHT YOU UP BY HAND!

DO YOU HEAR WHAT UNCLE PUMBLECHOOK SAID? BE GRATEFUL!

HAVE SOME MORE GRAVY, PIP!

Mrs. Joe is Pip's "shrewish" sister. Although Joe remembers when Mrs. Joe was a "fine figure of a woman," Pip has different memories of her: "My sister … was tall and bony, and almost always wore a coarse apron, fastened over her figure behind with two loops, and having a square impregnable bib in front, that was stuck full of pins and needles." Mrs. Joe makes a merit of having brought Pip up "by hand," although she says she would never do it again.

Pip imagines that he finds the love his sister will not give him in **Miss Havisham**. In his childish dreams, Miss Havisham is "the good mother," although Pip's first sight of her should suggest something else. Miss Havisham "was dressed in rich materials—satins, and lace, and silks—all of white." Pip looks closer, however, and sees that "the bride within the bridal dress had withered like the dress, and like the flowers, and had no brightness left but the brightness of her sunken eyes." As we learn, Miss Havisham lives in a frozen moment in time; she has stopped all the clocks at Satis House at twenty minutes to nine, the exact moment when her fiancé deserted her. In the course of the novel, Pip must accept that Miss Havisham is not his "good fairy god-mother;" her very name suggests her deception of Pip ("have-a-sham").

Characters

If Pip mistakes Miss Havisham for a fairy god-mother, he also believes that **Estella** is the "fairy princess" whom Miss Havisham intends him to marry. Pip's first impression of Estella is that she "seemed older" than himself, was "beautiful and self-possessed," and "was as scornful of [him] as if she had been one-and-twenty, and a queen." Estella is not a "fairy princess," but a cold human being whose heartlessness is the result of Miss Havisham's training. She says to Pip, "It seems … there are sentiments, fancies—I don't know how to call them —which I am not able to comprehend. When you say you love me, I know what you mean, as a form of words; but nothing more. You address nothing in my breast, you touch nothing there."

Although Pip wants to deny that he has any relationship with the convict he first met on the marshes, **Abel Magwitch** knows better. When Magwitch returns, he says, "Yes, Pip, dear boy, I've made a gentleman on you! It's me wot has done it! … Look'ee here, Pip. I'm your second father. You're my son—more to me nor any son." Magwitch certainly has more right to say that he's Pip's "father" than Pip has to say that Miss Havisham is his "mother." But Pip responds to Magwitch with "abhorrence," "dread," and a "repugnance" that "could not have been exceeded if [Magwitch] had been some terrible beast." Only when Magwitch is (safely) on his deathbed is Pip able to be genuinely affectionate and grateful to the man who has brought him up, not "by hand,"

but through love.

Dickens tells us that **Uncle Pumblechook** is a "well-to-do corn-chandler in the nearest town." A "corn-chandler" is a dealer in the seeds (or "pips") of cereal plants (like wheat, barley, oats, and rye).

"Brought up 'by Hand'"

When Mrs. Joe reminds Pip that she brought him up "by hand," she's not only referring to discipline (some would say physical abuse). She also means that she was responsible for keeping him alive as a baby. Pip's mother died when he was quite young, and without Mrs. Joe's efforts to spoon-feed him, he would have died as well. To understand Mrs. Joe's anger towards Pip, think about how much energy and patience it would have taken her to spoon-feed a small baby several times a day throughout its infancy. Mrs. Joe resents Pip for having been a burden to her.

In several ways, **Biddy**—who comes into the Gargery household after Mrs. Joe's "accident"—is the exact opposite of Estella. While Estella is "proud" and "very insulting," as Pip says, Biddy is "pleasant and sweet-tempered."

Herbert Pocket is the "pale young gentleman"

AS MAGWITCH SLEPT, PIP LOOKED ON HIM WITH MIXED EMOTIONS HE FEARED THAT AT ANY MOMENT, PURSUERS MIGHT BREAK DOWN AND TAKE THE MAN FOR HANGING AT OLD BAILEY PRISON...

SENTENCED TO HANG, MAGWITCH CHEATED THE ROPE BY DYING OF HIS INJURIES. PIP WAS AT HIS SIDE AT THE END ...

O LORD, BE MERCIFUL TO HIM, A SINNER!

whom Pip meets in Miss Havisham's garden and later, Pip's flatmate in London. Pip writes that Herbert "had a frank and easy way with him that was very taking…. There was something wonderfully hopeful about his general air, and something that at the same time whispered to me that he would never be very successful or rich." Later, when Herbert makes his fortunes in business, Pip wonders how he "had conceived that old idea of [Herbert's] inaptitude," and he wonders if "perhaps the inaptitude had never been in [Herbert] at all, but had been in [himself]."

Mr. Jaggers is the lawyer who tells Pip of his "great expectations." Jaggers is an obsessive hand-washer, and this obsession has everything to do with the sort of clients he defends:

> *He washed his clients off, as if he were a surgeon or a dentist. He had a closet in his room, fitted up for the purpose, which smelt of the scented soap like a perfumer's shop… [H]e would wash his hands, and wipe them and dry them … whenever he came in from a police-court or dismissed a client from his room.*

Wemmick is Jaggers's clerk. Although he plays a minor role in this adaptation of Great Expectations, in the novel Wemmick is one of Pip's closest friends. He's also the lord of his own Castle, the proud son of an "aged P.," and fiancé to Miss Skiffins.

Bentley Drummle, much to Pip's regret, marries Estella. Although the marriage proves to be a tragic one for Estella, Dickens suggests that it is ultimately responsible for Estella's ability to find her heart.

Compeyson, Magwitch's archenemy, has "no more heart than an iron file, he [is] as cold as death, and he [has] the head of the Devil." He's also much more important to the plot of Great Expectations than it might seem at first.

SECRET PASTS

After reading the Classics Illustrated adaptation of *Great Expectations*, you might have some questions: What is Miss Havisham's past and the source of her rage against the male sex? Who is the man who left Miss Havisham standing at the altar? Who is Estella and how was she brought into Miss Havisham's household? Why does Compeyson hate Magwitch enough to pursue him even to London? Although it's possible to tell the story of *Great Expectations* without posing these questions, the story is made richer and more understandable by filling in the details. And to do that, we need to go back several years before the events shown on page one.

Miss Havisham, the novel tells us, was the "spoilt child" of a father who "denied her nothing" after the death of his first wife. Eventually, Miss Havisham's father remarried and had another child, whom the novel only refers to according to his alias, "Arthur." This half-brother to Miss Havisham was "riotous, extravagant, undutiful—altogether bad," and squandered his inheritance after his father passed away. In order to regain his wasted fortunes, the villainous Arthur arranged that his friend, Compeyson, would pursue his half-sister, Miss Havisham, and profess his love for her. Compeyson swindled Miss Havisham out of a large portion of her own fortunes, split the money with Arthur, and deserted his "beloved" at the altar. "The day came, but not the bridegroom.

[Compeyson] wrote her a letter" that she received at twenty minutes to nine, the very time "at which she afterwards stopped all the clocks." Since that desertion, Miss Havisham has "laid the whole

MY NAME IS JAGGERS AND I AM A LAWYER IN LONDON. I WISH TO HAVE A PRIVATE CONFERENCE WITH YOU TWO.

"COMPEYSON WAS THE MAN, DEAR BOY, THAT YOU SEEN ME A-POUNDING IN THE DITCH. HIS BUSINESS WAS SWINDLING, FORGING, AND STOLEN BANK-NOTE PASSING.

The Setting

Although Dickens published *Great Expectations* in 1860-61, the novel is set in the years 1807-23. The novel is one of Dickens's few "historical novels." Clues to the novel's historical setting include the following: Joe is a blacksmith, a profession that was becoming outdated by the industrial revolution; the Hulks, old ships in which prisoners like Compeyson and Magwitch were warehoused until they could be sent abroad to British colonies, were closed by 1858; the one-pound notes that Magwitch delivers to Pip were not in circulation between 1826 and 1914; Pip takes the stage-coach, not the train, from his home town to London; in 1835, criminals like Magwitch would no longer have had to fear capital punishment (hanging) if they illegally returned to England.

[house] to waste … has never since looked upon the light of day," and only opens up her world to invite in children from the outside: Estella, the "pale young gentleman" in her garden (the young Herbert Pocket, later Pip's London flatmate), and Pip.

Although Compeyson is a minor character to the plot of *Great Expectations*, he's important because of his relationship with Miss Havisham and with Abel Magwitch, Pip's convict. Arthur, who was not in good health when he swindled Miss Havisham, died soon after the events described above. Compeyson was left to seek a new partner in crime; he found this partner in the young Magwitch. "Compeyson's business was the swindling, handwriting forging, stolen banknote passing, and such-like," Magwitch tells Pip, "All sorts of traps as Compeyson could set with his head, and keep his own legs out of and get the profits from and let another man in for, was Compeyson's business." Eventually Magwitch and Compeyson were convicted of forgery—"a charge of putting stolen notes in circulation"—and sent to prison. But Magwitch was outraged when he learned that Compeyson—because he pretends to be a "gentleman"—only received a sentence of seven years, while Magwitch himself received fourteen. The men have an ongoing, unrelenting hatred for each other, and Magwitch is obviously satisfied when he's able, at the beginning of our story, to deliver Compeyson over to the soldiers after his escape. "Now, the Hulks has got its gentleman again," he says with a sarcastic emphasis on the word "gentleman." In a final act of hatred, Compeyson alerts the police that Magwitch has returned to London.

And what of Estella? One of the most startling revelations of the novel is that Estella, Pip's "ideal" woman, is the illegitimate child of Magwitch and a woman named Molly, currently housekeeper to the mysterious Mr. Jaggers. Molly is described as "a young woman, and a jealous woman, and a revengeful woman," who was involved with Magwitch in his tramping days (before he met Compeyson). Several years before the novel opens, Molly became enraged when she learned of another woman's interest in Magwitch; several characters imply that she killed her rival. To complete her revenge, Molly confronted Magwitch and threatened to kill their small child, a girl: "On the evening of the very night when the object of her jealousy was strangled … the young woman

TRY, AND NOT DO IT? I TOOK HIM AND I GIVE HIM UP. I DRAGGED HIM HERE. NOW, THE HULKS HAS GOT ITS GENTLEMAN AGAIN.

[Molly] presented herself before Provis [Magwitch] for one moment, and swore that she would destroy the child (which was in her possession), and he should never see it again; then, she vanished." Molly "vanished" as far as the Old Bailey, a criminal court-house in nineteenth-century London where she was tried for murdering "the other woman," defended by the up-and-coming lawyer Jaggers. With Jaggers's help, Molly was found innocent. After the trial, Jaggers took her for his housekeeper; as for the child (whom Molly had hidden away, not killed), Jaggers felt that "here was one pretty little child out of the heap [of children in London], who could be saved" from a life of misery. He sent Estella to Miss Havisham, who wanted something to distract her from her unending grief over Compeyson's betrayal. There Estella is, as Herbert puts it, "brought up ... to wreak revenge on all the male sex." Miss Havisham seems to pick Pip as a lower-class training dummy for Estella to practice on as Estella gets ready to break the hearts of higher-class men (like Drumble) later in life.

YOU COARSE LITTLE MONSTER! WHAT DO YOU THINK OF ME NOW?

I SHALL NOT TELL YOU!

These character histories should give you a sense of the "thick relations" that hold between Dickens's characters, how the lives of characters continually cross and recross each other. By the end of the novel, it seems that the lives of Pip and Estella have crossed for the last time, and that there will be no further departures: "Then Pip took Estella's hand in his ... he saw no shadow of another parting from her." Dickens had originally planned a different ending for *Great Expectations*, which he only changed on the advice of friends. The final paragraph of this alternate version of the novel tells of Pip's final meeting with Estella, who had suffered "great cruelty" at the hands of Drumble, her husband. Pip explains:

I was in England again—in London, and walking along Piccadilly with little Pip [Joe and Biddy's child]—*when a servant came running after me to ask would I step back to a lady in a carriage who wished to speak to me.... the lady and I looked sadly enough on one another. "I am greatly changed, I know; but I thought you would like to shake hands with Estella too, Pip. Lift up that pretty child and let me kiss it!" (She supposed the child, I think, to be my child.) I was very glad afterwards to have had the interview; for, in her face and in her voice, and in her touch, she gave me the assurance, that suffering had been stronger than Miss Havisham's teaching, and had given her a heart to understand what my heart used to be.*

This ending shows, like the ending of the Classics Illustrated adaptation, that Estella has "now realized, too late, the value of [Pip's] love." Unlike the ending of the CI version, this ending holds no promise of a final union between Estella and Pip.

Gentility—Love, Not Money

Themes

The plot of the novel involves Pip's unexpected rise from "common laboring boy," as Estella calls him, to proper gentleman. Gentlemanliness—gentility—is a theme that runs throughout the novel. Although Pip believes that his entire happiness hangs on his ability to become a gentleman, the events of the novel ask us to question whether Pip's rise in status truly makes him happy. At the heart of the novel, of course, is Pip's realization that he became a gentleman not through Miss Havisham's efforts but through Magwitch's. This discovery forces Pip to re-evaluate his entire life and his past behavior to people like Miss Havisham and Joe. He feels like a fraud, his life as worthless as the forged bank-notes that Magwitch and

Compeyson put into circulation in their thieving days. But in what sense is Pip a "fake?" What did it mean to be a gentleman in the nineteenth century? How has Pip failed to be a proper gentleman?

There are basically two aspects to the idea of "the gentleman": a "moral" aspect and a "social" aspect. The moral aspect of gentility has to do with one's gentleness as a human being, and it focuses on one's sensitivity and kindness toward others. The social aspect of gentility has to do with one's social status, and it focuses on the family one comes from, the education one has received, the amount of property one inherits. Before the nineteenth century, these two aspects of gentility were considered inseparable: a gentleman was a man who was polite in his manners and privileged by his birth. But during the nineteenth century, things began to change. It became possible for a man who had earned his wealth through his own efforts to be considered a gentleman, regardless of his birth. The dictionary definition of "gentle" as "mild in disposition, or of well-bred manners; not stern, severe, or rude; kindly" comes before the definition of "gentle" as "of honorable family; distinguished by blood, birth, or station." Our idea that one's gentleness is less a matter of "birth" than of "disposition" comes from the nineteenth century.

Pip is a gentleman not because of his birth but

Violence

Great Expectations is a violent book, although you might miss the fact because of the emphasis on the romance between Pip and Estella. And most of the violence (emotional and physical) is directed at young Pip: Magwitch threatens to "have [his] heart and liver out," and stands menacingly over Pip with a drawn knife; Mrs. Joe beats Pip with the "tickler" while she makes Pip feel guilty for his very existence; Uncle Pumblechook humiliates Pip at Christmas dinner; Estella makes Pip feel "like a dog in disgrace"; later she slaps him; Miss Havisham plays with Pip's mind and encourages his belief that she's his benefactor; and Herbert, who doesn't even know Pip, challenges him to a fight in Miss Havisham's yard.

because of the "great expectations" showered on him by his unnamed benefactor—Magwitch. In the world of the novel, Pip is able to become a gentleman because the old rules no longer apply: he doesn't need gentle birth in order to be a gentleman. He can be made into a gentleman through either his own efforts or the efforts of another. Why is Pip so upset to discover that the source of his wealth is not Miss Havisham but Magwitch? Money is money, right? And what does it matter whether Pip's money comes from a decaying daughter of the upper middle classes (she's the daughter of a brewer, a "country gentleman," Dickens tells us in the novel) or a convict who earned his fortunes in an Australian penal colony raising sheep? The truth is that the source of Pip's wealth does matter—to Pip.

When Magwitch and Pip are first reunited, Pip recognizes Magwitch as "the convict he'd befriended many years before," but does not immediately understand that Magwitch is also his benefactor. He's embarrassed by the appearance of this low-life ex-con in his plush apartment, and he tries to persuade Magwitch to leave by reminding him of their social difference: "Understand that our ways are different and I cannot renew our acquaintance," he tells Magwitch,

YOU ONCE SENT A MESSENGER TO ME WITH TWO ONE-POUND NOTES. YOU MUST LET ME PAY THEM BACK.

before attempting to end their relationship by repaying the two one-pound notes Magwitch sent Pip as a child. Pip seems to be embarrassed by Magwitch because his lowliness reminds Pip of his own lowly origins. Throughout the novel, Pip turns his back on his home and original friends because he finds them "inferior." He tells Biddy that he's "disgusted" with his calling and his life at the forge, and although the CI adaptation states that Pip's "heart remained at home with Joe and Biddy" on his first trip to London, his two friends are not mentioned again until the end of the story—so much for family ties!

Pip would obviously prefer that his "great expectations" came from Miss Havisham, not Magwitch. He would prefer this not only because Miss Havisham's wealth comes from respectable sources, but because of his love for Estella, Miss Havisham's ward. In fact, as Pip tells Biddy, he wants to become a gentleman "on her account." Estella, however, will have nothing to do with Pip. In the beginning of the story, Estella calls him a "common laboring boy," and mocks his "coarse hands" and "thick boots." Estella is less rude towards Pip as he comes into his fortune, but because she was never given love as a child, she cannot now return love as a adult. Only at the end of the story, when she has been "bent and broken" through her disastrous marriage with Drummle (Dickens is explicit: Drummle beats her), does Estella "understand what [Pip's] heart used to be" and show any ability to love another human being. Estella's change of heart after her marriage matches Pip's change in fortune after Magwitch's death: the state has taken all of Magwitch's fortune, and Pip must start his life anew—not as a gentleman but as a clerk in Herbert's business ventures. Pip

and Estella are able to love each other only after Pip has stopped pursuing the status of gentleman, given over his fortune, and returned home to Joe and Biddy.

Orphans

There are three orphans in the novel: Pip and Estella, both of whom are major characters, and Biddy, a character who is minor (in terms of the number of her appearances) but important to the sense of the story. Beside the tombstones of Pip's parents, whom he never knew, are the tombstones of Pip's five brothers; Pip has been adopted by Joe Gargery and Mrs. Joe, but theirs is far a from happy household. Part of Pip's desire to improve himself comes from his desire to get out of his small town and out of reach of the "tickler" (the rod with which Mrs. Joe beats Pip). Pip wants to escape so desperately that he imagines he receives aid from the least likely people: around Miss Havisham, Pip dreams of an entire family to replace the one that he lost as a child— if Miss Havisham is his "mother," then Estella will be his "fiancée" and Mr. Jaggers his—well—strange "uncle." Of course, Pip's imaginary family actually involves Magwitch as his "father," Estella as his "sister," and Mr. Jaggers as his— well—strange "uncle." What the events of the story teach Pip is that he has to let go of both "imaginary families" and return to his "true family," which now consists of Joe and Biddy (Mrs. Joe has conveniently died). Although the CI adaptation of Great Expectations does not tell you this, the name of Joe and Biddy's small child is "Pip": "We giv' him the name of Pip for your sake, dear old chap," Joe tells his friend, "and we hoped he might grow a little bit like you, and we think he do."

Estella is also an orphan, adopted by

Miss Havisham as a small child and knowing no other family. But while Pip at least had Joe to ease Mrs. Joe's dehumanizing abuse, Estella had no one to protect her from Miss Havisham's influence. Even Pip understands that Estella has been trained "to wreak Miss Havisham's revenge on men." Miss Havisham only loves Estella—and it's a strange sort of "love"—as a pawn in her games. Is there more to Miss Havisham's love? After all, she seems truly shocked to learn that she has destroyed Estella's ability to love not only men but also Miss Havisham herself. "'O, look at her, look at her!' cried Miss Havisham bitterly; 'Look at her, so hard and thankless, on the hearth where she was reared! ... Did I never give her love! ... Did I never give her a burning love, inseparable from jealousy at all times, and from sharp pain, while she speaks thus to me!'"

The only lesson that Miss Havisham, as a "mother," has taught Estella, as her "daughter," is how to be an emotional stranger. Pip can at least return to Joe and Biddy as his "true family" at the story's end, but Estella has no family to turn to. Her only chance of family seems to lie in Pip's arms.

Biddy is the third orphan in the novel. "Biddy was an orphan like myself; like me, too, had been brought up by hand," Pip says. Of all three orphans, Biddy is the one most able to give and receive love in unconditional terms. By all rights, she should be the ideal woman for Pip, but because of his hankering for gentility and, later, his "great expectations," Pip only sees her as "common" and not like Estella.

Why does Dickens place an orphan at the center of his story? Why is he generally so interested in orphans? Part of the answer lies in Dickens's fascination with the effects of society on the individual, especially the child (Little Nell in *The Old Curiosity Shop,* or the heroes of *Nicholas Nickleby, Oliver Twist* and *David Copperfield*). Between society and the child usually stands the family, which gives the child its place and sense of self-worth. But the orphan is a child without a family at hand. The orphan does not immediately know its place—it has a hard time saying who it is in relation to those who surround it. Imagine how hard it would be to answer the questions, *who am I? who loves me? and why do they love me?* if you didn't have the support of a family. This is the problem of the orphan-child in Dickens's novels.

Of the three orphans in Great Expectations, only Biddy seems to be untroubled by her status as an orphan. She seems to know what her place is without much effort: it is alongside Joe in his home. On the other hand, Pip and Estella's ignorance of who they really are leaves them vulnerable to dangerous influences. Estella is completely taken over by Miss Havisham: she's only a toy with which Miss Havisham plays in her games of revenge against the male sex. Instead of giving himself over to someone else's control, Pip tries to find himself in the role of Miss Havisham's "gentleman." But since Pip's dreams for self-improvement turn out so miserably, are we to suppose that Dickens is saying that Pip's dreams are wrong in themselves? Is this the "moral" of the story? Should Pip have stayed at home with Joe, regardless of how much Mrs. Joe beat him or how often Uncle Pumblechook humiliated him? If we look closely, I think we can see that Pip suffers not because his dreams for self-improvement are somehow "wrong," but because they take him away from those who love him (like Joe) and make him want to impress those who do not (like Estella). Dickens is saying that we should try to better our selves and that we should do so in ways that honor where we come from.

•How is Dickens's dislike for the British class system shown in *Great Expectations*?

•Can Pip's efforts to become a "gentleman" in London can be seen as a betrayal of his friendship with Joe at the forge?

•Why does Magwitch "adopt" Pip? Why is his gratitude to Pip strong enough to cross two continents and several years? What are the reasons he gives in the story? What reasons can you come up with?

•Why would the lawyer Jaggers feel the need to wash his hands after dealing with Pip and his "great expectations"?

•Think about the theme of the "secret life" in *Great Expectations*. What are the connections between Pip's life as a boy from the laboring classes (a life that he keeps secret from others) and Estella's life as the only daughter of a convict and accused murderess (a life that others keep secret from her)?

•Consider the violence in *Great Expectations*. Why does Dickens go to such lengths to make us feel that Pip's life is constantly threatened? How is Pip's wish to be a "gentleman" in London related to his sense of being always at risk in his home town?

•Consider the relationship between Pip and Magwitch. Why does Pip insist on their difference from each other? How are they similar to each other? Remember what Magwitch says: "Look here, Pip. I'm your second father. You're my son..."

•Think about the "moral" of *Great Expectations*. What is the novel's message about Pip's desire for self-improvement? In your opinion, is Pip more of a "gentleman" with or without his fortunes? In what sense of the word? Support your opinion with references to the story.

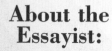

HERBERT AND PIP BECAME VERY SUCCESSFUL ABROAD. PIP KEPT IN CONSTANT TOUCH WITH JOE, BUT IT WAS ALL OF ELEVEN YEARS BEFORE HE RETURNED TO HIS OLD HOME FOR A VISIT. THEY SPOKE OF ESTELLA...

TELL ME, AS AN OLD FRIEND, HAVE YOU QUITE FORGOTTEN HER?

I HAVE FORGOTTEN NOTHING IN MY LIFE THAT HAD A PLACE THERE... BUT THAT POOR DREAM, AS I ONCE CALLED IT, HAS ALL GONE BY.

About the Essayist:

Michael Doylen is a doctoral candidate at the University of California at Santa Cruz, where he is affiliated with The Dickens Project, a national consortium of sixteen colleges and universities that focuses on the work of Charles Dickens.